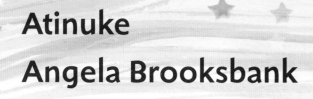

Baby, Sleepy Baby

Atinuke
Angela Brooksbank

For our Swedish Akinyemis with love ~ **A**

*For sleepy babies everywhere and to those
who love them so dearly* ~ **AB**

CANDLEWICK PRESS

This book was typeset in Shinn. ✿ The illustrations were done in mixed media.
Candlewick Press, 99 Dover Street, Somerville, Massachusetts 02144 ✿ www.candlewick.com
Printed in Humen, Dongguan, China ✿ 21 22 23 24 25 26 APS 10 9 8 7 6 5 4 3 2 1

Baby, sweet baby,

I'll call on the winds

and you'll sail like a ship
through the sky.

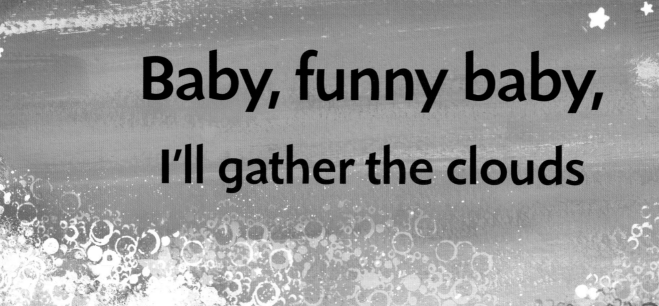

Baby, funny baby,

I'll gather the clouds

to cuddle you,
cozy and close.

Baby, happy baby,

I'll sing down the stars

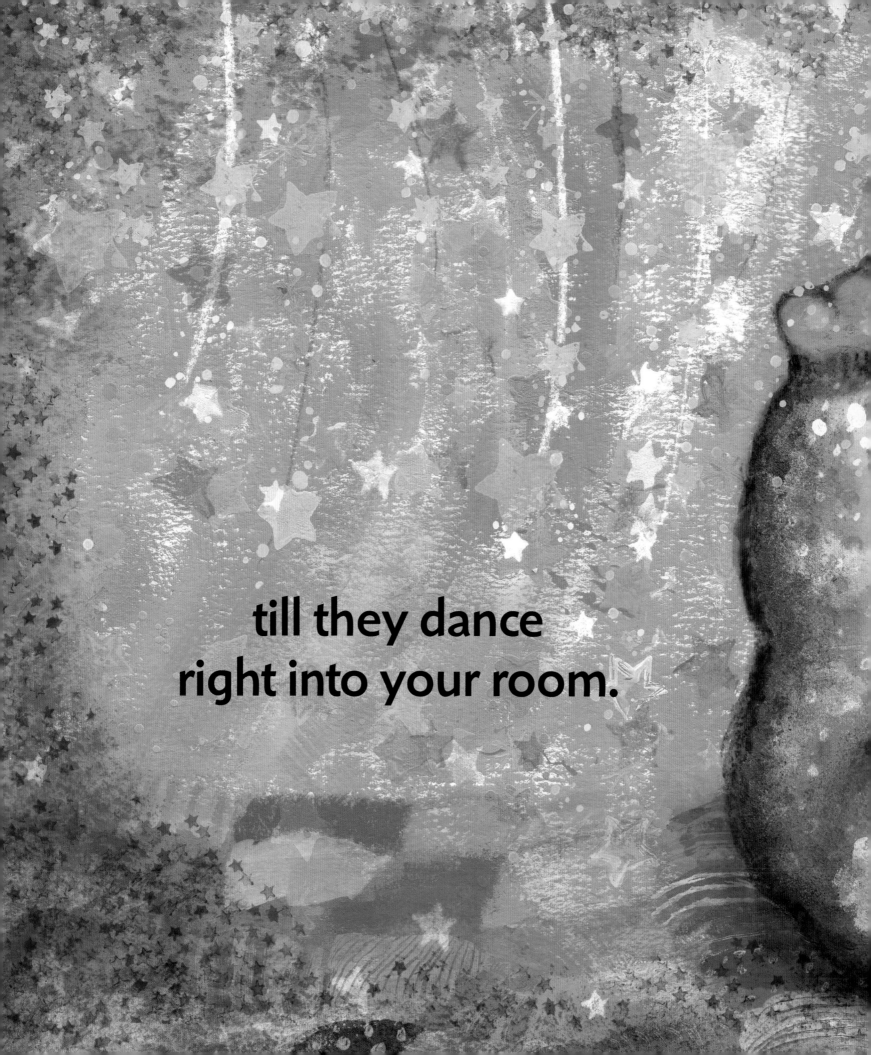

till they dance
right into your room.

Baby, dear baby,
I'll beg of the moon
to smile on your sweet,
chubby face.

Baby, lovely baby,

I'll pull down the black sky

to wrap you in night's
soft blanket.

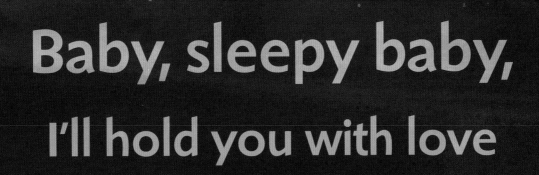

Baby, sleepy baby,

I'll hold you with love

as softly we drift
among dreams.